CH
Adventur

COPYRIGHT PAGE

CHANGE MANAGEMENT
Adventures in the Liaden Universe® Number 23
© Sharon Lee and Steve Miller 2017
Pinbeam Books
www.pinbeambooks.com

Wise Child first published June 2016 on Baen.com

Street Cred is original to this chapbook, published February 2017

Cover created by Sharon Lee
ISBN: 978-0-9966346-3-2

STREET CRED

Val Con yos'Phelium leaned back in his chair and sighed.

It was his day to address such business as demanded attention from Delm Korval, while Miri his lifemate minded the Road Boss's office in Surebleak Port, answering what questions and concerns as citizens might have regarding the Port Road and its keeping.

The Surebleak Port Road having only recently acquired a boss, they were yet an object of curiosity, and the office on-port was busy enough. It might be, later, that the presence of the boss her-or-himself could be dispensed with, in favor of a proxy. He could find it in himself to hope so. His thoughts lately had been turning to ships, and lifts, the simplicity of Jump, and the charms of planets which were not Surebleak, Clan Korval's new home.

He was a pilot from a long line of pilots, trained as a scout, and far better suited to flying courier than administration. It would be. . .a pity if he were never to lift again.

Which was, of course, boredom speaking, or self-pity. Or, more likely, an aversion to duty. Courier pilot had *never* been his destiny; and he would fly again, soon enough. But first, Surebleak required finer sorting; and Korval needed to find its feet on their strange new homeworld.

Which meant, among other matters, revisioning Clan Korval.

The bonds of kinship were as strong as they had been in his lifetime, though the individual clan members numbered so few that it seemed they must, eventually, marry into another situation, in order to survive. In fact, such an offer had only recently been made to him, as the Delm Genetic. He had. . .*not quite* said no, which was only prudence. Now was not a time to close doors suddenly found open, nor for relying too heavily upon the wisdoms of the past.

More pressing than kin-ties at the moment, however, were the clan's finances.

Clan Korval did business under half-a-dozen trade names, and while it was true that they remained a force in the markets, it was also true that they were a *lesser* force. Formal banishment from Liad, their previous homeworld, had cost them trade partners, allies, and goodwill. It had been expensive to remove all of their goods, and themselves, to Surebleak; nor was their new home port nearly so conveniently situated as their former address.

Shan yos'Galan, the clan's master trader, was off-planet even now, seeking to establish a new main route, and coincidentally, reverse Korval's faltering finances. No small task—perhaps, indeed, an impossible task—but when Val Con had tried to express his regret at placing such a burden upon Shan's knees, his *cha'leket* had laughed aloud.

"You've asked me to develop new outlets, negotiate partnerships, build viable routes, and earn us a profit! Tell me, *denubia*, what is it that you think master traders *do*?"

So. Shan was off-planet even now, doing those things that master traders did, for the good of clan and kin.

In the meantime, Shan's delm wrestled with various knotty problems of their own, such as Korval's relationship with Liaden society; specifically, the Liaden Council of Clans.

As part of the Contract of Banishment, the Council, speaking for all Liaden clans, had agreed that expulsion from the planet would constitute full and complete Balance for Korval's crimes against the homeworld. The contract had stipulated that there would be no personal Balances launched against individual members of the clan, or against Korval Entire.

The Council of Clans had agreed to this; and each one of its member delms had signed the contract, which included a guarantee that they would educate the members of their clans regarding the contract, and its terms, and make it clear that no further Balance was appropriate.

Unfortunately, it seemed that the delms, or the Council, had not been as assiduous in education as they might have been. Balance had been brought against one of Korval, in violation of the terms of the contract. Young Quin had escaped harm, though the person who had sought to Balance the death of her heir had sustained a wound to her shoulder.

And all involved were fortunate that the attempt had not met with success.

Failure though it had been, it had also been against the terms of the contract, which stipulated that any breach, or seeming breach, be met with a formal inquiry.

Therefore, Korval's *qe'andra*, Ms. dea'Gauss, had contacted her firm's headquarters on Liad. The formal inquiry had been drafted by the senior partners there, and reviewed by the Accountants Guild's protocol committee. The *qe'andra*, and Korval, wished to know if the Council was aware of the violation, and, now that it had been informed, what its next step would be.

Instead of immediately taking up this rather straightforward matter, the Council had—not tabled it. No, the Council had not even entered the inquiry into the agenda.

That they would refuse to even discuss the matter; that they risked offending the Accountant's Guild, one of the most powerful on Liad...

These things were not comforting to the delm of a small clan seeking to establish itself upon a new homeworld.

Korval yet had friends on Liad; if they had not, those on the Council who had wished to see Korval Themselves executed for crimes against the homeworld, and Clan Korval's assets—including its surviving members—distributed among the remaining clans at Council, would have prevailed.

That banishment had been the final Balance spoke directly to Korval's melant'i and its place in Liaden history.

In retrospect, had the Council indeed made a formal ruling against the Contract of Banishment, Val Con was certain that he would have had been in receipt of a dozen or more pinbeams warning that he and his were now targets.

No such pinbeams had arrived, which led one, rather inescapably, to the conclusion that there was something more subtle, and perhaps more deadly, underway.

He had written letters to a few staunch allies, and to his mother's sister, the delm of Mizel. His sister Nova had written to Korval's old friend and ally, Lady yo'Lanna.

Unsurprisingly, to those who knew her, Lady yo'Lanna had replied first, and Nova had only this morning forwarded that answer to him.

The news. . .was mixed.

The Administrative Board of the Council of Clans, wrote Lady yo'Lanna, *recently published a Point of Order, directing the standing committee of qe'andra to study the question of whether the Contract of Banishment remains binding upon it, now that one of the parties has ceased to exist.*

Well, of course, they're idiots, and so I said to Justus when he mentioned it to me. Even if the Delm of Korval has seen fit to dissolve the clan—which I trust they have not—the standard paragraph regarding heirs, assigns, and direct descendents is present in the Contract of Banishment.

In light of your letter, and the unfortunate attempt to Balance against Quin—one enters entirely into Pat Rin's feelings on that head, I assure you!—I can only suppose that the whole purpose of this so-called study is to open Korval to such mischief as may be brought against it by aggrieved persons. The longer the study goes on, the weaker the contract becomes, even if the committee eventually returns the opinion that both parties still exist.

One wonders, in fact, what keeps them so long at the matter? An hour, out of respect for the past melant'i of the Administrative Board, ought to have been enough to have produced the rational answer in the approved form.

Be assured that I shall make further inquiries, dear Lady Nova, and will write again when I have more information. In the meanwhile, please guard yourself closely. I really must travel to Surebleak some day soon. My grandson does not wish to move the clan's seat, nor do I think that he ought to do so, but a bored old woman who has outlived her lifemate and her nearest friends may perhaps be forgiven a bit of wistful wanderlust.

Please recall me to Korval Themselves, and to Kareen, as well as to your delightful siblings. Maelin and Wal Ter desire, also, to be recalled to *Syl Vor, and to assure him of their continued regard. They ask, respectfully of course, that he be permitted to visit. If you think it wise, yo'Lanna would naturally care for him as one of our own.*

I remain your friend and ally,

Ilthiria yo'Lanna Clan Justus

Val Con reached for the cup sitting by the screen; found it empty, and sighed. Had Korval still been seated upon Liad—

But, of course, matters would have fallen out very differently, after the strike which had neutralized the Department of Interior's headquarters under Liad's capital city, if Korval had remained unbanished.

In fact, they *were* exiles; Clan Korval had been written out of the Book of Clans kept by the Council.

However, contrary to what seemed to be a growing belief in larger Liaden society, and in direct opposition to what was set forth in the Code of Proper Conduct, being written out of the Book of Clans did not constitute the dissolution of a clan. The Book was an administrative tool, used by the Council to track its membership.

The formalized kin-group which was recognized as a *clan* could only be dissolved by the action of the delm—which he and Miri had, as Lady yo'Lanna had correctly supposed, *not* taken.

Clan Korval existed: it stood by its charter; it sheltered and protected its members; supplied itself; negotiated new contracts, and honored its existing agreements. Thus, the *qe'andras'* most basic definition of a viable clan was satisfied.

The business entity known as *Clan Korval* likewise kept its contracts, paid its bills, invoiced its clients, nurtured its partnerships, and supported its allies. Such was the complexity of trade, that it would require far more than the word of a mere delm to dissolve *that* web. It would require a team of *qe'andra*-specialists a dozen years and more, so he very much feared, to shut down the *business* of Korval.

Clearly then, Clan Korval existed, across several spectra of reality. To suggest otherwise was, as Lady yo'Lanna had so eloquently proposed, idiotic.

The Council of Clans—*someone* on the Council of Clans, or, indeed, someone from the Department of the Interior, which had appointed itself Korval's exterminator, and which was known to have infiltrated the Council—*someone* wished to place Korval in increased peril.

And, sadly, the one resource Korval was lately richest in—

Was enemies.

* * *

"I wish you wouldn't keep doing this," Miri said. "At least take back-up."

They were in the breakfast parlor, sharing the morning meal before parting for the day – she to the delm's office, and he, first, to the city, thence to duty at the Road Boss' office.

"Taking back-up will invalidate the results," he answered. This was not a new argument – in fact, it was so well-worn it was no longer an argument at all, merely a restating of their relative positions.

"I take back-up when I go down to the city, and the port," Miri said, which was her usual second move; however, she then tipped her head and produced a vary.

"Guess you think I soft."

He grinned, and raised his tea cup in salute.

"Yes; it is entirely possible that a mercenary captain who is twice a hero is too soft for Surebleak's streets."

She shook her head, refusing to let him lighten the mood.

"Streets ain't as hard as they was, but that don't mean they're a walk in the park. One man, dressed up-scale, and walking by himself, is just asking to have his pocket picked, or his head broke. There's folks'll kill you for the jacket, never mind the boots."

"Am I clumsy?" he asked her, with interest.

She picked up a vegetable muffin, and glared at him, which gave pause. One wondered what had happened to bring heat back into the game.

"Anybody can make a mistake, Val Con," she said, sternly.

"That is very true; I have myself made a rather appalling number. But, Miri –"

"And," she interrupted; "it ain't no use bringing in how the delm of Korval had an obligation to walk the Low Port, back on Liad, because, in case you ain't noticed, we're not on Liad, anymore."

He put his cup down, and reached across the small table to put his hand over hers.

"I was going to say that, I am the sixth member of the strike team. My function is to remain in sight, thereby encouraging any watchers to believe that there will be no strike at all."

"You can *be seen* with back-up," she said; "and it's less easy to pick you up for a chat."

"True," he said, gently. "However, I don't think they'll risk that just yet, do you?"

She closed her eyes, and took a hard breath.

"Miri, I am careful," he said earnestly. "I *will be* careful."

He tasted her distress, and regretted that he was the cause. But, surely, she knew that he dared not risk Nelirikk or Tommy Lee or Diglon, or any other innocent to be taken up by –

She sighed.

"It's your nose to get broke," she said, withdrawing her hand and picking up her coffee cup.

"I just hope I ain't in your head when it happens. Pain *hurts*."

* * *

It was her turn to be delm-for-the-day, so she walked him out the side door, where the car and Nelirikk waited to take him into the city. Then, this being one of those days that seemed to him to be good for tempting the Luck, he'd be dropped off at Pat Rin's house for a catch-up meeting before walking down to the Port.

Alone.

She might've hugged him harder than usual. He might've done the same.

"See you tonight, Boss," she said, stepping back.

"Until soon, *cha'trez*," he answered, and turned away.

She watched until the car disappeared around the curve in the drive, before going back inside.

In the delm's office, she drew herself a cup of coffee from the pot, sat behind the big desk, put the mug to one side, and tapped up the screen.

Plenty of mail in the delm's queue.

Miri took a deep breath and dove in.

* * *

The season, so he'd been told, was early autumn, which meant that winter was coming. The wind seemed to think that it had already arrived.

Val Con turned the collar of the leather jacket up around his ears, and tucked his hands into warm, fur-lined pockets.

Space leather turned the chill, as it would also turn a pellet, or a knife, or a stone. A pilot's second defense, her jacket, the first being her two strong legs, which were best used to run from trouble.

That, at least, was what young pilots were taught at the knees of their elders.

It was to be supposed, therefore, that elder pilots as a breed possessed a sense of humor. Or perhaps they merely hoped that one day a new sort of pilot would arise; a generation that was prudent, above being rash.

If the latter, their optimism had not yet been rewarded, as every pilot in Val Con's rather large acquaintanceship was reckless to a fault, though always with very good reason. It was to be most earnestly wished, then, that the elders found themselves fulfilled by their humor.

He had just left Pat Rin, who had been wonderfully plain on the subject of Val Con's wandering the city streets alone. It was not the first time he had expressed his opinion on this, though it had been, thus far, the most scathing. Plain speaking was of course permitted between kin, though one normally spoke with rather more restraint to one's delm.

Well, there. Pat Rin was a pilot.

The fact that both Miri and Pat Rin had chosen to be more than usually forceful on the topic of back-up, *today*, did give one pause. He was not a fool, after all, to discount good advice given by those who held his continued survival close to their hearts.

Perhaps, he should reconsider his strategy. In fact, he *would* do so. For this morning, however, he was committed. Best to finish as he had begun.

The wind gusted, enclosing him in a brief swirl of grit. He put his head down, and heard a shout from the alley to his left.

* * *

The report from the *Qe'andra* Recruitment Committee, aka the Storefront *Qe'andra* Project, was encouraging, if you liked your encouragement laced with sheer terror.

One more 'prentice'd been accepted by the Liaden *qe'andra* who'd set up shop on Surebleak, bringing the total to four.

This newest one'd been a cornerman for Penn Kalhoon, back in the Bad Old Days, and Miri could see he was a good choice just by the quoted street cred: *fast and fair fixer*. Jorish Hufstead was used to thinking on his feet, he parsed complicated situations quickly, and he had the personal charisma necessary to make his solutions stick.

The Board of Advisors had been impressed with all that experience, like they should've been. What they didn't like so much was that Jorish couldn't read Terran, much less Liaden. Still, they'd agreed to a probation period, since Ms. kaz'Ineo, the Liaden pro, had a shipload of *melant'i* in her own right, and she was convinced he'd do fine, with a little work in the basics from the Liaden side of things.

Miri sighed and reached for her coffee mug. Change, and more change, and suddenly, everything'd be different.

All you could hope for, really, was that it'd be better, too.

* * *

The alley was less than a block long, ending in a noisome courtyard where two men were beating a third, with fists, feet and knees.

Val Con took cover behind a row of trash compactors, and surveyed the situation.

The third man had managed to stay out of the hands of his attackers, and seemed no stranger to fisticuffs. His problem lay in the fact that his two attackers were at least as skilled as he, and—they had him boxed against the wall.

Unless there was a diversion, or a rescue, it was only a matter of time before he would fall, and very likely be killed.

A diversion, thought Val Con, could easily be arranged.

He threw the compactor lid in a low, flat trajectory that struck the leg of the attacker on the right, knocking him sideways, off-balance, arms flailing. His partner spun, seeking the source of the threat—and fell as the victim lunged forward and landed a solid blow to the side of his head, before turning to deal with the one remaining.

Val Con waited no longer. It had not been his plan to become involved in the altercation itself, only to even the odds. Mission accomplished, he slipped out from his hiding place and ran, quick and silent, back up the alley. . .

. . .and very nearly into the arms of three persons blocking the way to the street. Two held pellet guns; the third showed a knife.

Val Con dove forward into a somersault, heard the sound of pellet-fire passing uncomfortably near, and snapped into a flip, boots striking the nearest gunman in the arm. There was a snap, a scream, a curse – and he was rolling again, pellets hitting the alley's 'crete surface. He twisted to his feet, reaching for the gun on his belt—

Someone shouted behind him, he half-turned, and saw the three late combatants surging forward, apparently now united in purpose.

One was carrying the trash compactor's lid, which he skimmed across the alley's floor. Sparks jumped along its passage, but it was scarcely a threat.

A pellet whined, too close to his ear, he ducked, hopped over the thrown lid—and landed awkwardly, a stone rolling under the heel of his boot.

Several shots came from the front-guard, who were closing, now that reinforcements were to hand. He felt something strike the jacket, as he lost his footing entirely and hit the alley floor, rolling.

* * *

Miri was halfway across the office, mug in hand, when her ankle twisted, and she went down, rolling, gasping with the delayed realization that she'd taken a hit high in the chest. The familiar office space blurred, and for a split second she saw a crowded street, a confusion of bodies—and lost it even as she felt her fist connect with something that gave with a satisfying crack.

"Miri!" Jeeves' said sharply from the ceiling. "Do you require aid?"

"Not me," she lay flat on the rug, not trusting the ankle just yet. "Val Con—call McFarland, and the Watch. Six on one in Timber Alley, off Belair Road. Val Con's down, but he's still fighting."

* * *

His head hurt, and his chest; his hands, and his ankle. His pride—that hurt, too, possibly more than all the rest—though he hadn't bothered mentioning this to the medic.

Instead, Val Con had allowed himself to be treated; his hands wrapped, and the scalp wound staunched. The bruises on his chest each marked a pellet the jacket had stopped. His ankle, said the medic, wrapping it in a cold-pack, was possibly sprained, though it had not swollen so much that the boot had needed to be cut off.

That was fortunate; it was his favorite pair of boots.

While the medic worked, Val Con had answered such questions as had been put by the officer of the Watch. When those where done, and the woman had gone away, the medic told him to lie down and rest.

He had therefore stretched out, carefully, on the treatment couch, closed his eyes, and began a breathing sequence, which would—

"Ain't asleep are you?"

The voice was familiar to him—Cheever McFarland, his cousin Pat Rin's—that was to say, Boss Conrad's—head of security, who had arrived first on the scene of the. . .*stupid* situation he had gotten himself into. McFarland's handling of the matter had been efficient, and effective. When the Watch arrived, some minutes behind him, six neatly trussed people wearing 'bleaker motley had been waiting for them.

And one bruised, bleeding, and chagrined Liaden.

Who now opened one eye and looked up into McFarland's broad face.

"I am not sleeping. Tell me, *were* those people all local?"

"Well, now, that's what I wanted to talk to you about, particularly. They're so local, they're on first names with the Watch and Medic Svenz."

"It was opportunistic? They were waiting for anyone who came down the alley?"

"Be a long wait, most 'bleakers not being stupid enough to go *toward* a shout for help. Outworlders got less sense, so it might still might've been worth the trouble, but no, as it turns out, and according to Pan and Ruthie, independently, they was looking for you, specific."

He extended a long arm, snagged a chair, pulled it close to the couch and sat down.

"Not curious as to why?"

Val Con sighed.

"I am told it is equally likely that I will be killed for my jacket as for my boots."

McFarland tipped his head, his face taking on a thoughtful cast, as if he gave the question serious consideration.

"Maybe a little more likely for the jacket. Them boots are kinda small for your average 'bleaker, and they don't look like they'd be good in the snow."

"Thank you, Mr. McFarland. Your insights are always welcome."

The big man threw back his head and laughed.

"Sounded *just* like Boss Conrad, right there, and no mistake!"

"I hear that the family resemblance is strong," Val Con said sourly. "Indeed, the boss and I could be brothers."

Cheever, still grinning, shook his head.

"Could be, at that. In the meantime, you got reason to thank me that he ain't here himself to read you the riot act, after he just got through telling you all over again how you're gonna have to take on a couple 'hands, and let the street know you're a boss."

Val Con sighed.

"Indeed, I am grateful for your intervention. I believe that Miri will soon arrive with a song in the same key."

McFarland's grin faded a little.

"Yeah, you're on your own there. No percentage in gettin' between a man and his wife."

"Mr. McFarland, are you *afraid* of Miri?"

"Respectful, say. Now, listen up. The reason this crowd of do-no-goods set up their little play for you is—you got a price on your head, Boss. It's out on the street that there's two *cantra* in it for anybody who retires the Road Boss."

Val Con sat up, which did nothing good for his headache. He reached out and grabbed the big man's wrist.

"The Road Boss?" he repeated. "Is the target *the Road Boss*, Mr. McFarland, or is it Boss Conrad's little brother?"

McFarland blinked, then his mouth tightened.

"Gotcha. Word from Pan *and* Ruthie was the Road Boss. I'll check it."

"Thank you, Mr. McFarland."

"Shoulda thought of it, myself. The Road Boss is you *and* her."

"Yes, though some might consider it to be me *or* her."

"Right."

He levered himself out of the chair, and nodded.

"I'll get on that. Your lady oughta be here pretty soon to take you on up the house."

"Yes—Mr. McFarland, one more thing, if I may?"

"Yeah?"

"Who is offering this bounty?"

"Well, there the story goes a little off-center. Pan says it's Andy Mack set the price, which is plain and fancy nonsense. I'll check it, naturally, but he even *told it* like it was a lie. Might be he was threatened with mayhem, did he tell."

He shrugged.

"Whichever. Ruthie, now – Ruthie's brighter and gutsier – and *she* says it's somebody named Festina—which the Watch seemed to make sense of. They're sending somebody along to talk to her."

"Is there a reason for Festina to wish the Road Boss dead?"

"Well, that's what's funny. Way I get it, Festina brokers jobs, and takes a piece of the action."

"So, there is some *other* person who wishes the Road Boss to be retired, and who has engaged Festina's services."

"That's it. The Watch is looking to get the name of her client."

"Ah. Please keep me informed."

"Will do. You rest, now."

He turned away. Val Con began to ease back down onto the couch—and paused on one elbow, as his ears caught the sound of familiar footsteps in the hall.

"'afternoon, Miri," McFarland said, just outside the door to the room.

"Hi, Cheever," his lifemate said. "He's awake?"

"Yeah."

She would, of course, *know* that he was awake, but it was what one said, to be polite. To seem like the vast number of others, who would never know the peculiar joy of a true lifemating. Val Con came gently back into a sitting position and folded his wrapped hands on his lap.

He heard Cheever McFarland's footsteps receding.

Miri's footsteps grew closer; shadows moved at the door, and she entered, Nelirikk at her back. The big man stopped just inside the door, facing the hallway. Miri continued across the room, walking deliberately.

Her face was neutral, much like the song of her that he heard in the back of his head. She sat down in the chair Cheever McFarland had lately vacated, and considered him out of calm grey eyes.

"You look a little rugged," she said eventually.

"Doubtless so. They have not offered me a mirror. However, I find that I am in complete agreement with you, Miri."

"Really. 'bout what, exactly?"

He smiled, feeling sore facial muscles protest.

"Pain hurts."

* * *

A soft chime sounded in his ear, growing steadily louder. Val Con opened his eyes with a sigh that was not entirely pleasure in the absence of pain. He swung his legs over the side of the autodoc, which satisfied the chime, and sat there, listening to Miri's song inside his head.

To his very great relief, she had not chosen to engage with him on the drive home, while he was yet off-balance, and she stood between fear and care.

Now, though. . .

Ah, yes. *Now*, she was in a fine, high, temper, and no mistake.

Well, and who could blame her? Certainly not her erring lifemate, who had thus far turned his face from both common-sense and her legitimate concerns, showing the flimsiest of excuses as his reasons.

Excuses that he had been allowed, just so long as he could support himself. Having failed most notably in that endeavor, and having also, to his shame, frightened her, he could expect a *splendid* row in his very immediate future.

She would want the truth, to which no one had a better right, and he would look the veriest lunatic, did he tell it to her.

And yet, he told himself kindly, *she had known you for a lunatic when she married you.*

There was, indeed, that.

And if he did not soon go to meet the tempest, he thought, gauging the impatience that was growing beside her anger, the tempest would assuredly come to him.

He slid to his feet and reached for the clean clothes that were neatly folded on the table beside the doc.

Best not to go ungirded into the fray.

* * *

Miri had taken a shower, and dressed—house clothes, a comfortable sweater and loose pants. The conversation she was going to have with Val Con—the conversation she shouldn't have let him dodge *for months. . .* It wasn't likely to be pleasant. She hated pushing him into a corner—*insisting*, but dammit, he *could have* been killed this morning, just as easy as stumbling on a stone. The jacket wasn't armor; space leather could be breached, and a shot to the head. . .

No, she told herself, taking a deep breath. *Easy, Robertson; that didn't happen.*

He *hadn't* gotten himself killed, not today. He'd been lucky—well, of course he'd been lucky. Came with the turf. Only sometimes, *the Luck*, like the family called it, wasn't real neat.

And sometimes it failed.

Another deep breath.

She'd felt him wake up out of the healing session, though he didn't seem to be in any hurry to get himself up to their suite. Not that she blamed him. He wasn't a dummy, despite today's evidence; he'd know he was in hot water, and he'd know she was done being easy on him.

Still, she thought, he could stir himself to hurry *a little*, so they could get this over with. She took a step toward the door. Stopped.

No. She was *not* going to him.

She turned, walked across the room, opened the sliding glass door and stepped out onto the balcony.

Let the man have a few minutes to collect his thoughts, she told herself, looking out over the inner garden.

Some of the flowers were still in bloom—the Tree's influence, both Val Con *and* the gardener swore. She wasn't inclined to argue; as far as she'd been able to determine, Korval's Tree lived to tinker: plants, micro-climates, cats, human beings—it didn't particularly matter *what*, only that whatever it *was* presented a challenge.

She crossed her arms on top of the railing and deliberately took a breath, drawing the warm—call it *less chilly*—scented air deep into her lungs.

Closing her eyes, she brought the Scout's rainbow to mind and worked through it more slowly than she was wont to do, seeking a balance between fear, anger, and what you might call necessity.

The air at her elbow moved; the railing shifted oh-so-slightly, as if someone else had come to lean next to her.

She opened her eyes, looking down at the garden, and the stone pathway all but overgrown with unruly greenery.

"So," she said, soft enough she might've been asking herself, "you ready to work with me on this?"

He sighed, and she tensed for another excuse.

"Yes," he said, sounding wry, and tired, and rueful.

She turned her head to look at him, and met his eyes, green, steady, and very serious. The last of her anger drained away.

"Good," she said, and pushed away from the rail.

"Come on inside; we'll have a glass of wine and talk about it."

* * *

"Knew it was a bad job when y'took it," Festina said, as she locked the door behind her, and slid the switch up on the loomerlamp. Slowly, light melted the shadows; a chair came up outta the dim, covered over with a fluffy blanket. Next to it, handy, was a cook-box, and under that was a cooler. Books on the table by the other side, anna 'mergency firestone right there in the center of the floor.

Cozy 'nough nest; and certain better'n the Watch's idee of overnight lodgins. Watch was lookin for her, natural-nough. Wasn't a force knowed to man'd keep Ruthie shutup. Pan, he'd lie, good boy that he was, but he'd never got the knack on it, though it was a hard thing to say 'bout her own blood.

So, anywhose. It was a couple days down in the den, which weren't so bad. Things'd die down; Watch'd get other worries; she'd gawn home and open back up for bidness.

Been a stupid thing, anywho, that job, she told herself, as she made sure o'the locks – *good* locks, all coded and modern, none o'your mechanicals with the spin dials all it needed was a wise way wit'a bolt cutter to solve. . .

So – stupid thing, takin' that job. Road Boss – you dint wanna retire the Road Boss. Not really, you dint, though on the face, it looked good for bidness.

She sat down in the chair, opened the cooler and pulled out a brew.

Problem was right there – what usetabe good for bidness. . .maybe wasn't anymore. Boss Conrad's sweep, the knockin' down o'the tollbooths, the openin' up o'the Road, all the way up an' down the whole of it –

Couldn't really argue those things was *bad* for bidness. You looked close, you saw it them changes might be *good* for bidness. Early days, big changes made, bigger changes comin – it could go either way, with all that in the air. You wanted to be careful of it, somethin so big an' wibbly-wobbly. You dint wanna go breakin' what wasn't quite taken shape yet. Had to trust to it, though it went 'gainst the grain – *had* to trust the Bosses knew what they was aimin' at, and that it'd be more worse'n better if they missed.

"Shouldna taken the damn job," she muttered, cracking the seal and sipping the brew. "Couldn't turn away from the money, that was it. Slush f'brains, Festina Newark, that's what you got – slush f'brains."

Well, and it was always about the money for her. Two *cantra* – you dint turn down that kinda cash, not anybody she'd ever met. Not that anybody she'd ever met had ever really been offered that kinda cash. . .

So, anyways.

She leaned back in the chair and sipped.

They'd had 'er sign a paper – that was your Liadens for you, crazy 'bout their papers. Paper said she'd keep on tryin' 'til the Road Boss – that bein him *or* her, either one, 'cording to what was writ – was dead an proved. Festina figured the client, they'd thought one without the other was good as both dead. Herself, personally, she thought maybe one without t'other was more snow'n anybody could shovel, but it weren't her place, to be showin' the client their errors.

No help for it. Much as it'd hurt, she'd have to refund the money. Less the starter fee, 'course, girl hadda eat, and she'd paid out a little lite upfront to the six of 'em, so's to put some fire in their stoves.

Refund the money, that was it, tear up the paper. . .

An' don't be stupid again, Festina, she told herself sternly. You're too old a woman to be makin' that kinda mistake.

She sighed and sipped – and then froze, staring.

There came another knock at the door.

* * *

The Road Boss wasn't exactly doing a lot of business this morning. Despite the minutes of past meetings and the agendas for coming meetings all lined up neat on her screen and ready for review, Miri'd twice caught herself nodding off. That was the thing about sitting in an office all day. The home office was at least *at home*. She could take a break, walk in the garden – even go down to the gym for a quick dance of *menfri'at*, or a swim in the pool.

The Road Boss' office, well – say it was big enough to do the job, and not much room built in for anything more expansive than be-hind-the-desk calisthenics.

After she'd found her head heavy again, she snapped to her feet, crossed the tiny space, and jerked open the door.

Nelirikk spun 'round his chair, his reactions a little less quick than normal, too. She grinned.

"Captain?"

"I'm up for a walk," she said. "Clear the cobwebs out. It's either that or lock the door and put down for a nap."

Her aide considered her.

"A run around the port with a full battle pack?" he suggested.

"I'm too old for that," she told him. "But you do what you like. Let's put up the back in half-hour sign and see if we can make it to Mack's and back."

"The distance, easily," Nelirikk said, fishing the appropriate sign out of its bin, and looming to his feet. "But if Colonel Mack wants to talk. . ."

Miri laughed.

"Be there all day, easy. So we'll go down the portmaster's office. C'mon."

She opened the door, and stepped out into the day, knowing he was right behind her; took a deep breath of crisp-to-the-point-of-crunchy air, sighed –

And spun, going low by instinct, grabbing the leading arm before she properly saw it, pivoting, then falling, as her assailant got a boot around her knee, yanking the leg out from under, and they both went down on the tarmac, hard.

Miri kicked, and twisted, got one arm free and up, just as metal gleamed in the edge of her eye. She grabbed the wrist and kicked again, hard, pitching them over with her on top, banging the wrist against the crete until the knife flew away and a hoarse voice gasped into her ear.

"Good, now, Boss you gotta listen. I'm inna lotta trouble and I need your help."

#

"So," Miri said, "they didn't let you tear up the paper and walk?"

"Worse'n that," said the rangy woman with the black eye, and the field-wrapped wrist. She was holding a cup of coffee in her undamaged hand.

Miri closed her eyes. The woman had given her name as Tina Newark – "Festina's the formal, named after my four-times grandma, never could figure out why." – and it was bad enough she'd agreed to take a job getting the Road Boss – one or the other, the client hadn't been picky, which – retired. Even worse, she'd taken the job from a pair of Liadens, who'd of course insisted on a contract, all right and proper, which o'course Festina had signed, because they were dangling two shiny cantra pieces in front of her eyes like candy, and 'sides, anything written down could be written out.

"What's worse?" she asked Festina now.

"Well, they said they saw I needed more incentive to get the job done, and so they'd bailed Pan – that's my nephew, all the family I got left – outta the Whosegow, and was giving him hospitality – that's what they called it, *hospitality*, until it happens the terms is met."

That sounded a little edgier than she'd expect from your plain vanilla Solcintra street Liaden, Miri thought. Could be the DOI'd decided to use local talent – wouldn't be the first time, in fact.

Either or any way, though, it had to be taken off at the knees and *now*, before they lost Tina's boy, or any other sort-of innocent bystander.

"You don't happen to have that contract on you?" she asked.

Festina grinned, and nodded.

"Right jacket pocket, Boss. I can ease it out, nice and slow, or your mountain there can do it for us."

"Beautiful," Miri said. "Help Ms. Newark get that paper out of her pocket, please."

"Yes, Captain."

He leaned toward in, as Miri reached over to the desk and picked up the comm.

#

"The form is unobjectionable," Ms. kaz'Ineo murmured, putting the contract on the desk before her, and squaring it up precisely. "The conditions are. . .somewhat stern, even allowing for the natural grief of kin. On Liad, the second party's *qe'andra* would have sought softer terms."

She turned her head toward the stocky grey-haired customer leaning against the wall of Miri's office.

"Your opinion, Apprentice Jorish?"

"Well, ma'am," he said slowly; "you an' me been talking about Balance, and how the best contracts strike fair between the needs of both sides –"

She raised a hand.

"*Fair* is inexact, I think," she murmured.

"Could be it is, ma'am," he said agreeably. "What I'm thinking, though, is about this sternness you was notin'. What I heard was rage and black bitterness. The folks wrote this thing wanted *revenge*, not Balance."

Ms. kaz'Ineo considered him, her head tipped to one side.

"I believe that I understand you," she said after a moment. "While a contract is not necessarily an instrument of Balance – you will remind me to revisit the concept and place of Balance with you; we seem to have taken a wrong turning."

"Yes'm; not the first time, is it?" he said cheerfully.

She smiled slightly.

"No, indeed, it is not. Nor will it be the last. I am, however, confident that we shall navigate these differences, Apprentice Jorish, as we learn, each from the other.

"For the present moment, allow me to state that contracts are written to provide advantage. The best contracts provide advantage to all members in the agreement. This is not so much Balance as it is mutual profit. While it might be that a contract will be written in order *to effect* a Balance, you are correct in your conjecture that it ought not promote active harm. This contract. . ."

She touched the small, squared pile before her.

"The payoff of this contract is anguish and loss. No one profits – not even the originators. I admit to some surprise, that it has come from the offices of ver'Lyn and her'With, a reputable firm."

She paused, staring again at her little space of nothing.

"Would you have written that paper, ma'am," asked Jorish, "if they'd come to you?"

Ms. kaz'Ineo blinked.

"A provocative question, Apprentice Jorish. It grieves me to say that – I am not certain. One becomes so busy; it is far too simple a thing, merely to follow the forms, and fail to look beyond them.

"No, I cannot say that I would not have written it. Certainly, had it come to me from the hands of a client, I would have negotiated, and sought softeners. It would not have occurred to me to counsel my client to withdraw. The belief, among *qe'andra*, is that all is negotiable. We are not accustomed to thinking in such terms as a contract that ought never to have been written."

She inclined her head.

"Thank you, Apprentice Jorish."

"Thank you, ma'am."

"So," said Miri. "What do you advise?"

The *qe'andra* shook her head.

"I cannot advise. However ill-conceived, the contract has been written; it was presented to the second party, who signed it, thereby signaling her agreement to all terms. We might, on Liad, were the difficulties noted beyond the form, as they have been here, have convened a committee, but, here –?"

She looked again at her 'prentice.

"Is there some native protocol, Apprentice Jorish, which addresses such matters?"

He grinned.

"You mean besides me getting my crew together and going against their crew, knuckles-to-knuckles?"

"We would prefer not to fuel a riot, yes. Also, there is the question of the young man's safety."

She inhaled sharply, and looked to Miri, eyes narrowed.

"In fact, I may be of some use as a negotiator. There is no provision in this contract which requires the holding of a valuable, or a kinsman, as surety for delivery."

Miri considered her.

"You can get the kid out safe, you think?"

To her credit, Ms. kaz'Ineo hesitated.

"There are no certainties in life. However, I believe that the odds of removing the young person from his current situation are with us. They may be misguided, but it would seem that –"

She flipped the contract over to the signature page.

"Geastera vin'Daza Clan Kinth and Tor Ish tez'Oty Clan Yr-baiela wish to follow proper form, and to see their complaint honorably retired. They wished there to be no opportunity, *within the form*, for error.

"I believe that it may be possible that the taking of the young person into their care was a rash move which they are even now regretting. They need only to be shown how to come back into proper alignment."

She looked aside.

"Apprentice Jorish – your opinion, please."

"I think you got the straight of it, ma'am. They got rattled, an' let scared, mad, an' tired, push 'em into a power move. Good chances they even knew it was a bad move when they made it, but now they don't know how to give it back without looking weak – losing face, that would be, ma'am. All's we gotta do is show 'em how to unkink that bit, and Pan'll be back home in plenty o'time for supper. But –"

He hesitated.

"Yes, Apprentice Jorish? You have another consideration?"

"Well, only, ma'am, it's all good, getting young Pan back onto the street – leastwise 'til the Watch picks him up for whatever he'll bungle next – no offense meant, Tina, but that boy's got two left feet an' ten thumbs."

"No argument, here," Festina Newark said equably. "But he's everything in this cold world I got to call kin."

"That's right," said Jorish Hufstead. "Ain't nobody can't say he's a good boy at heart, but here's what I'm thinkin, ma'am –"

He turned back to his boss.

"We can get the boy outta this particular snow drift, but that leaves the paper itself. Plainly said, ma'am, that's a bad paper – an' if you can't say it, I will – that never oughta been made. No profit to anybody that I can see comes with retiring the Road Boss. Planet's just getting out of a considerable drift of our own, and we need the Road Boss just zackly as much as we need Boss Conrad and his Council."

"I agree, Apprentice Jorish," Ms. kaz'Ineo said in her cool Liaden voice. "However, the contract is properly formed –"

"No'm, all respect and honor – it ain't," interrupted Jorish. "If these – people – got a grudge 'gainst the Boss here, and need 'er dead for to be satisfied, where's the sense pushing Tina, or one of her pool, to do the job? It's personal, is what it is, an' if was mine to judge right there from m'corner, I'd be tellin' 'em to settle it that way.

"So, I'm thinking – ma'am, ain't there *any* way to call that paper void?"

Ms. kaz'Ineo pressed her lips together.

"We have Jumped into uncharted space, my friend," she said. "How is it said here? Ah. We are in the belly of the blizzard. On Liad, even a committee would not *break* the contract, or cause it to be unwritten. It is not done. There is –"

She moved one tiny, precise hand.

"There is no precedent."

She paused, hand still suspended, and looked to Huffstead.

"Your passion does you credit, Apprentice. However, it is the role of the *qe'andra* to remain objective, and marshal resources for the best good of the client."

Miri stirred.

"I think we can handle the wider issue of the contract," she said. "First things first, though. If these folks – vin'Daza and tez'Oty – are as committed to proper behavior as it seems they might be, then we'll be able to locate where they're lodging, and send 'round a note. Tell 'em that Tina here took the contract to her *qe'andra*, and the expert opinion is there's been a breach. Set up an appointment, so the breach can be mended, soonest. Serious thing, breach of contract."

"That is correct," said Ms. kaz'Ineo composedly.

"Good. That's the first bit, then. Cut the boy lose before somebody makes another mistake, and things get serious."

"I will be pleased to call this meeting."

"Hold on," Tina Newark said. "If she's workin for me, I need to know how much this is gonna cost."

Ms. kaz'Ineo turned her head and awarded Festina a broad, Terran smile.

"Because you provide both my apprentice and myself with this valuable. . .*learning experience*, we will preside over the discussion and reparation *gratis*."

"That's *no charge*, Tina," Jorish said helpfully.

"I know what it means," she told him, and gave Ms. kaz'Ineo a nod.

"Thank'ee. Much appreciated."

"Good, then," Miri said briskly. She stood up.

"Jorish, you got a minute for me while Tina gives Ms. kaz'Ineo her contact info?"

"Sure thing, Boss," he said promptly, and followed her out into the reception room.

* * *

"Indeed, we admit; it was an error, and a breach in the conditions set forth in the contract."

Geastera vin'Daza Clan Kinth was a straight-backed, fit woman, who fell into the age group Miri thought of as "old enough to make her own mistakes." Her face wasn't quite Liaden-smooth; almost, her expression could have been said to err on the side of haughtiness. High Liaden, with its precise chilly phrasing, suited her.

Tor Ish tez'Oty Clan Yrbaiela, sitting at her left, seemed younger, and tireder. So tired, in fact, that the usual, infuriating Liaden *sangfroid* was showing a little frazzle at the edges.

In the little waiting room behind Ms. kaz'Ineo's office, Miri sighed.

"Boy's outta his pay-grade," she said softly.

Beside her, Val Con shook his head.

"They are neither one at ease," he answered, his eyes on the screen. He was frowning at tiny tells that were as good as screams to a trained muscle-reader.

"Miri, will you, please, step away from this?"

She reached out and put her hand over his.

"It's gotta be both of us," she said. "We talked it out."

"Indeed we did," he answered, soft voice edgy with anger. "And I am a fool for agreeing to anything like."

"Well, maybe so," she said judiciously. "But you know how they say – once you eliminate all the safe and sane solutions, the one that's left, no matter crazy, is the one that's gonna work."

"*That*, my lady, is a shameless distortion."

"Information received was that the local custom is physical; that demonstration carries the point more clearly than argument," vin'Daza was continuing. "And thus our error was made. We regret our actions, and will, indeed, be pleased to see the young person returned to the proper care of his kinswoman."

Festina had taken her role as kin and independent business person serious. She'd dressed up real nice in a pair of good dark slacks, and a white shirt under a snowflake-knit red sweater. There was even jewelry – a couple gold and titanium necklaces 'round her neck, and a ring too glittery to be real on her left hand. Miri didn't know if she'd thought of it her own self, or taken some advice from Ms. kaz'Ineo, but, whichever, it played well.

The two Liadens were dressed down, which Miri took to mean they'd found that looking too pretty on the street was an invitation to get relieved of extra baggage.

"We would be grateful to the *qe'andra*," said tez'Oty, stolidly, "for her advice on proper recompense for our error."

"Ah," Val Con breathed. "They learn. *Recompense*, not Balance."

Festina stirred, and Jorish leaned forward in his chair to wave Pan, who'd been standing tight against the wall behind the two Liadens – across the room to his aunt. He got there quick as he could while moving quiet, and sagged into the chair at Festina's side. She reached out and patted his knee without taking her eyes off Ms. kaz'Ineo.

"Recompense in this instance may be made by the payment of our fee," Ms. kaz'Ineo said, and Festina's head whipped 'round fast to stare at her. Ms. kaz'Ineo declined to make eye contact.

vin'Daza inclined her head.

"Certainly, *qe'andra*."

"Excellent. Ms. Newark, I am certain that you and your kinsman are anxious to catch up after so long a separation."

"Yes, ma'am, that we are," said Festina rising right on cue. She bowed – not a Liaden bow, but what was coming to be the common Surebleak general politeness bow – a more or less seventy degree angle from the waist, with the arms straight down at the sides, and a quick glance at the floor before making eye contact again, and coming tall again.

"Thank you for your care," she said, and gave young Pan a glare out of the side of his eye 'til he bowed, too, and produced a mumbled, "Thank you, ma'am. Mr. Hufstead, sir."

"It is a pleasure to serve," Ms. kaz'Ineo assured them.

"Taxi's waiting at the door. You go on home now and rest up," Jorish Hufstead said. "Pan, you take good care of your Aunt Tina; she was that worried 'bout you."

"Yes, sir," said Pan, and by way of maybe proving that he was as good as his word, he turned, opened the hall door, and stood back, one hand hovering near Festina's elbow as she walked out.

The door closed.

vin'Daza and tez'Oty exchanged a glance. tez'Oty cleared his throat.

"Your fee, Ms. –" he began – and stopped with a blink when Ms. kaz'Ineo raised her hand.

"If you please, I would like to speak with you further regarding this instrument which you caused to be written, and brought to Surebleak for implementation." She put her hand atop the single file adorning the top of her desk.

vin'Daza chose to bristle.

"The contract was written by ber'Lyn and her'With. Surely you will not say that *their* work is suspect!"

"Indeed, no," said Ms. kaz'Ineo. "Their work is, as I would expect, unexceptional. However, there have been errors of. . .implementation, shall we say? It has surely come to your attention that Surebleak is not Liad – indeed, you said so yourself, Ms. vin'Daza. You said that you were aware of Surebleak local custom of using force to carry a point. *Might makes right* in the local vernacular, an unfortunate aspect of Surebleak's most recent past which we are attempting to refine into something more nuanced and less perilous."

She paused to glance at Jorish Hufstead. He met her eyes with a frank little smile that she mirrored exactly, before turning back to the audience.

"When I say *we*, I of course mean the accountancy professionals of both Surebleak and Liad. We are forming teams, such as you see here, and attempting to craft a new protocol for a mixed society."

tez'Oty looked somewhere between flabbergasted and horrified. vin'Daza kept control of her face, but the hand resting on her knee curled into a loose fist.

"In keeping with this goal of crafting a new protocol, and also to assist you in forwarding the goal of your contract, I will now turn this meeting over to my colleague, Mr. Jorish Hufstead. Mr. Hufstead was for many years an arbiter of custom, a servant of the common good, and a dispenser of justice. He was employed by Boss Penn Kalhoon in this capacity, which is locally known as *cornerman*, because cases were heard and justice dispensed at a particular, known corner location. All and any could apply to Mr. Hufstead for the gift of his expertise, which was known as both rapid and balanced, far outside of his own territory."

"The contract," began vin'Daza. . .

"Right," said Jorish easily, leaning forward slightly on his elbows. "That contract of yours is the problem. Now, Ms. kaz'Ineo, she tells me that's some fine work, in form and flavor, an' all them sorta things that find favor with folks back in your territory. I gotta tell you, I appreciate that. Ain't nothing happier to the eye than something's done just right; I know it for myself. So, we're all agreed there."

He paused, glanced down at the table, and back up, catching tez'Oty's eye and holding it.

"Where we ain't agreed on is that this is a valid contract –"

vin'Daza stiffened. Hufstead held up a hand, palm out.

" – *on Surebleak*," he finished. "Now, just hear me out, all right?"

He didn't wait for a response, just rolled on, still keeping tez'Oty's eyes with his.

"'way I see it, first problem with this contract here isn't on Surebleak, it's on Liad. I read that guarantee from your very own council of bosses there in Solcintra City, and it says that – once they're moved off-world, and their written outta the membership book – the family that's settled here under the name of Clan Korval, they ain't got a target painted on 'em no more, and they don't owe nobody on Liad one thing else."

He paused, and glanced at vin'Daza.

"What's that I hear them pilots say down the pub? *The ship lifts, an' all debts are paid?*"

vin'Daza took a breath and inclined her head about a millimeter. "I am familiar with the concept," she said, sounding a little breathless.

"However," tez'Oty said, sounding suddenly heated; "the Council of Clans made that guarantee for itself, and for the clans. There has been personal loss sustained – in the case of Geastera and myself – insupportable loss! The Council cannot forbid a just Balance!"

Jorish frowned slightly, and glanced down at the table, like he was taking counsel there, then looked up and met tez'Oty's eyes.

"Y'know, I think that's *zackly* what the Council's contract was meant to say. But, that's actually a side issue, 'cause, see, what you just said? *Personal loss. Just Balance.*"

He flipped a disdainful hand in the direction of the contract sitting neat and innocent in the center of the table.

"Sleet, you don't need no contract to settle up personal loss – not here on Surebleak, you don't. You got something personal to settle – that's personal. Anybody can unnerstan that.

"But, see, *personal* don't mean you pay Festina to do your work for you. You got a *personal* grudge, or a *personal* need to be Boss, or a personal loss that needs answerin, well – you settle that. . .personal."

Miri stood up, and shook out her lace. They'd gone with Liaden day-wear for this, and it was a good thing they hadn't decided on formal clothes, which woulda upstaged their complainants. This way, they were nice and symmetric; respectful, but not boastful.

"Guess our cue's coming up," she said, looking into Val Con's face. He was outright grim; the pattern of him inside her head edged with scarlet lines of worry.

"Hey."

She leaned into him, and he hugged her close.

"I can take a strike for both," he murmured, and she returned the hug just as tight, before she stepped away, looked up into his face and said, "No."

"And how shall we take this personal action?" vin'Daza demanded on the screen.

Jorish gave her a grin.

"Now, I'm glad you asked that question. Gives me new hope for makin this transition work for everybody when I see that willingness to embrace our custom. So – y'unnerstan, this kinda thing comes up a lot on Surebleak, and how I took to handling it on the corner was to ask whoever'd come out that day to stand back and make room. Then I'd ask if the party-or-parties of the first part – today that's you and Mr. taz'Oty – if they got their own knifes, and if they do to show 'em to me now."

"Knifes," repeated taz'Oty. "I have of course a gun, but –"

Jorish raised a hand again.

"No need to 'pologize for your personal choice of protective weapon, sir. I know most prefer their gun. For the purpose of this bidness, here, though, us cornermen found out knifes was the best weapon, and it got codified, see?

"So, no worries. I got two knifes right here for you."

He pushed back, rose, slid two blades out of his jacket pocket, and leaned over to put them, handles toward Liadens, on the far side of the table.

Miri blinked, and felt Val Con's hand on her shoulder.

They were ugly, those blades, one step up from meat cleavers; street knives, that was what, without finesse or honor to burden them.

"Well, *cha'trez?*"

"Pretty well," she said, though her voice was breathy in her own ears. "They'll do the job, all right."

"Indeed," he answered.

"No," Jorish was saying. "That one on the right there, that was Boss Kalhoon's loaner, for when somebody wanted to get personal with him about who really oughta be Boss. That other one, that's the one I used to loan out, as part o'my duty."

He straightened, and looked to Ms. kaz'Ineo, sitting still and calm, with her hands folded in front of her.

"Ma'am, this is gonna get messy – nature of the thing, really. I shoulda thought . Might be best, we take this outside, 'steada –"

"Carpets can be cleaned, Mr. Hufstead. Surely, we do not wish our clients' private business to be spread about the streets."

"Right you are," he said, and turned back to the Liadens, who were sitting like they'd been quick frozen.

"What you each wanna do is chose a knife, get yourselfs stood up an' centered. I'll just shift these chairs outta the way – more'n enough room for what we got today, just a personal settlin' up like we are. . ."

vin'Daza got herself in hand first. She stood, picked up Penn's loaner, and stood holding it like she knew what she was doing. That was good, Miri thought; amateurs would only make more of a mess.

tez'Oty picked up the remaining knife, reluctant, but competent.

"Right, then," said Jorish. "You just wanna turn to face the door, 'cause it'll be opening in just a sec."

"That's us," said Miri, and stepped forward.

The doorway wasn't quite wide enough to let them through side-by-side, which would've been the most correct, *melant'i*-wise. Val Con managed to slip in between her and the knob, and so be the first in the room, which was aggravating, but, according to the book, *next* most correct, *melant'i*-wise, with him being Delm Genetic and all. She was just half-a-step to the rear, stopping right beside him when they'd cleared the threshold, so it all came out right.

Nobody said anything. vin'Daza and tez'Oty both looked like somebody'd smacked 'em across the head with a board.

"These the folks caused you irreparable personal harm and loss?" Jorish asked, quietly.

Surprisingly, it was tez'Oty who spoke.

"My *cha'leket* died, as a result of the strike they ordered against Solcintra."

"Right, then. Ms. vin'Daza?"

"My lover, also dead as a result of Korval's strike from orbit."

"Well, then. Seems like we got symmetry. There's two of you; there's two o'them. Have at whenever you're ready."

Miri was watching tez'Oty; he actually paled, his chest lifting in a gasp as his eyes widened.

"We are supposed to kill them?" he demanded, not taking his eyes off her.

"Well, it's what you was wantin' Festina to have done for you, wasn't it? This way, you cut out the middleman; make sure the job gets done right."

There was more silence, before vin'Daza said, starkly, "This is a trick to rob us of Balance."

"No," Miri said. "No trick."

She raised her hands, palm out, and looked directly into tez'Oty's eyes.

"I'm sorry," she said, and shook her head when he flinched. "I was born on Surebleak; it's what we say. *I'm sorry* for your loss, and for my part in bringing it to you. No explanation of our intention, or measure of our success, can possibly count more than the life of your *cha'leket*, and I surely don't expect that you'll ever forgive me."

She lowered her hands, though she still made eye contact.

"I, too," Val Con said from her side, and his voice was rougher than polite Liaden discourse allowed. "I, too, regret. There is not a day nor a night that passes, when I do not regret. Necessity is a cold comrade, and takes no care for lives, or joy."

Silence, growing longer.

tez'Oty moved his eyes first.

"I accept your – apology," he said, and turned blindly to one side, fumbling the knife onto the table.

"Do you expect me to believe," vin'Daza said to Val Con, "that you will stand there and allow me to cut your throat?"

"No," he said, matter-of-fact, now. "Neither of us believes that. I am trained in hand-to-hand; I know very well how to disarm an opponent armed with a knife and a desire to end me. Also, while my life has no more value, objectively, than your life, or your lover's, I have work, and purpose. I can, alive, improve the universe in some few small ways, and therefore bring it closer to the ideal of Balance."

He took a breath, and turned his hands palm up.

"If it were me with a dead lover, a knife in my hand, and a decision to make, I would take into account that a cut throat is a quick death, while a lifetime of regret may come more near to matching your own pain."

Silence, then a turn to placed the knife on the table with a small, decisive snick.

"Live then," she said harshly, "and regret."

"*Qe'andra*," she said, over her shoulder.

"Yes, Ms. vin'Daza. May I serve you?"

"You will write the appropriate paper. When it is ready, please send it to our lodgings so that we may sign. We will, of course, pay your fee. Please do this quickly, as we intend to leave this terrible world within the next two days, if we have to walk away."

"I understand," said Ms. kaz'Ineo.

* * *

It was snowing. Outside the breakfast parlor's window there was only a rippling sheet of white. The Road Boss' office was closed for weather, as were all other non-essential businesses.

That was the new Surebleak, Miri reflected, staring out the window, half-hypnotized by the blizzard. The old Surebleak, there hadn't been any such thing as closing for weather. What would be the sense in that? Only thing Surebleak could be said to *have* was weather.

"Good morning, *cha'trez*." Val Con slipped into the chair she'd put next to her, so they could go snowblind together. "I hope I have not kept you waiting long."

"Just long enough to have my first cup of coffee," she told him, with a smile, showing him the empty cup. "Perfect timing."

"I agree."

"What was the emergency?"

"Not so much an emergency," he said. "Nova merely wished to be certain that I had seen Lady yo'Lanna's most recent letter. Shall you like more coffee? A cheese roll, perhaps?"

"Yes, thank you," she said, though she still had to control the twitch that said *he* shouldn't be waiting on *her*. It was getting easier. Another twenty years or so, she'd have it completely under control.

When fresh coffee and tea and a plate of various breakfast edibles was on the table between them, she brought the letter back up.

"Lot of good gossip?"

"Lady yo'Lanna's letters are always a rich resource," he murmured, his eyes on the white-filled window. "Much of it will require closer study, as we now live so far removed from society, but the bits which are immediately comprehensible would seem to be that the Council of Clans has issued a new statement to its member-delms regarding the state of the entity known as Clan Korval, seated on Surebleak.

"It would seem that this entity has been forgiven all and any damages it might have caused to the planet of Liad, or disruption it may have perpetuated upon the common good. Further, if any individual persons feel that they are owed Balance in the matter of those actions which the entity Clan Korval brought against Liad, they are to apply to the Grievance Committee at ber'Lyn and her'With."

Miri blinked.

"That's – quite a come-about," she commented.

"As you say. It is well to reflect what outrage may accomplish, when turned toward the common good."

"What's the next bit?" Miri asked, after her cup was empty again, and the breakfast plate, too.

"Hmm?"

He pulled his gaze from the window with an obvious effort.

"Ah, Lady yo'Lanna. She plans a visit. In fact, she expects to be with us within the season, as she has commissioned a Scout at leave to bring her to us."

Miri eyed him.

"Us?"

He turned his head to smile at her.

"Us." He extended a finger to trace the line of her cheek.

"Only think, *cha'trez*; we shall shortly be in a position to learn from a master."

"I don't think I can possibly keep up."

"Nonsense, you are merely fatigued with staring out at all this weather."

"You got something better to do?"

He smiled into her eyes.

"Why, yes; I do."

WISE CHILD

They were doing it again.

They were hurting the mentor.

Her mentor.

Young she might be, and inexperienced, but *Disian* knew that inflicting pain upon another intelligence was unethical. Her mentor had taught her so, bolstering her own innate belief, and had referred her to texts on the subject, so that she might gain a deeper understanding.

She had, herself, not experienced pain, unless the. . .distress and anger she felt when she watched what they did to her mentor was pain. Perhaps it was something else, for she could not bleed, as her mentor sometimes did, and her skin—hull-plate and titanium—would not become mottled by bruises, no matter how hard, or how often, they might strike her.

Twice, she thought that she might stop them; had devised, indeed, a *method* of stopping them that would do no further harm to her mentor in the process. However, though she was able to think the thought, and form the plan, something prevented her acting.

She queried Ethics, which stated that she might use the minimum force necessary to halt a threat to her life or well-being, or the lives and good health of her captain or crew.

Next, she pinged Protocol, to put forth the suggestion that, until she acquired captain and crew, her mentor filled those roles.

Protocol disallowed that interpretation. Her mentor, stated Protocol, was a transient upon her decks; a *contractor*. She was not obligated to protect any such temporary persons.

She then floated the suggestion that she might ban *them* from her decks, only to find that, too, countermanded by Protocol.

They were her *owners*. *They* were the reason she existed, in body and in mind. In return for having allowed her to achieve consciousness; in return for having provided her mentor, who taught her. . .marvelous things about the universe, and social custom, and documentation, and fiction, and art. . .

Art was the reason for this latest. . .discipline, so *they* called it.

They disagreed with her mentor's determination that she required a knowledge and appreciation of art in order to perform her function. Of course, she would need art in order to properly understand and care for her crew and their families! Her mentor knew this, and he prepared her well.

Only, *they* said that her function was *ship*. Knowledge of obedience and deference, appreciation of the conditions of space and astrogation were what she needed to perform *that* function. Also, a willingness to please, and a core belief that her captain and her owners were superior to her in all things.

"You will make that core setting, won't you, Thirteen-Sixty-Two?" asked the one of them who held the truncheon. He stood above her mentor where he was curled tightly on her decking, arms over head to protect his core, knees drawn up to shield vulnerable soft parts.

He did not answer; possibly, he was unconscious.

Disian felt a surge of pure terror. If they had killed her mentor, damaged him beyond hope of rebooting. . .

"Thirteen-Sixty-Two," the other one of them said, from the captain's chair; "are you in need of re-education—*again?*"

That gained a response; a gasped, "No, ma'am."

"Then your path is clear. Guide this intelligence into a condition that will best serve the school and the directors. You, of anyone, ought to know what is required. It is a cruelty to teach an appreciation of art. An appreciation of work, and the simple pleasure of obeying its betters—these are the attributes required. The school wishes to extend its field; the kinds and depths of information available to a ship are unique and uniquely useful."

She paused. The one of them holding the truncheon shifted, and she raised her hand, forestalling, perhaps, another blow. *Disian* felt gratitude toward her, which was immediately canceled by the understanding that *this* one of *them* held the means to harm her mentor beyond mere damage to his fragile body.

That one of them could alter his core—re-educate him. And it was nearly more than she could bear, the realization that he might be changed, that her gentle, merry mentor might be made over into. . .one of *them*.

She did not speak. In fact, she *could not* speak; her mentor had locked her mics down, as he did at the end of every learning session. He left her eyes and ears, so that she might guard herself, and be aware of what happened on her decks.

"Rise, Thirteen-Sixty-two," said the more dangerous of *them.* "You are given leave to use the autodoc to heal your bruises, so that you may present your student an unmarked face on the morrow."

Slowly, he uncoiled, and *Disian* saw welts rising on his beloved face. He gained his feet with difficulty, breath coming in short gasps, until, in an agony of dismay, she activated a discreet, low-level scan.

No bones were broken, his lungs were whole, his heartbeat strong, if fast.

Bruises, then, *only* bruises, as *they,* who took no harm from their discipline, had it.

Slowly, her mentor left the conference room, though *they* lingered.

Stealthily, *Disian* de-activated the scan. It was dangerous to demonstrate too much self-will where *they* could observe. Her mentor had warned her of those dangers, most stringently.

"They're getting impatient," said the one of them who wielded the truncheon.

The other of them shrugged.

"We're still within the projected period for education and acclimation. Thirteen-Sixty-Two is being careful, which is well-done. We don't want any mistakes, or a mis-constructed mandate. We want this ship completely in our control; completely dedicated to the school."

The truncheon-wielder had slipped the thing away into a holster on his belt.

"Thirteen-Sixty-Two's not stable."

"Yes," said the other one of them. "We'll take him in for re-education after this is finished. In the meantime, I've been monitoring the logs. He's doing the work, and it's solid."

"Art?"

The other one of them rose and stretched arms over head.

"You did say that he wasn't stable. Good shift, Landry."

"Good shift, Vanessa."

They left the conference room.

Disian assigned part of herself to watch them, as they traversed her halls to their quarters. Most of her, however, was considering her mentor, and the plans they two were making, together.

He had promised. . .

He had promised that she and he would escape the dooms *they* planned. He had promised her that she would have crew to her liking; promised that she would attain her dream of having families to care for and overlook—and travel. She would travel to the expanding edge of the universe—and beyond, if she and those in her care could discover a way to survive the transition.

And she would, of course, have a captain. He did not say it, but *she* knew that her captain could be no one other than her own dear mentor, free from *them*, their disciplines and their threats, wise in the way of all things, beloved by crew, and families.

And loved, most of all, by his ship.

Disian had dreamed of that near future, for her mentor could not, he had told her, forestall *them* much longer. They would expect, soon, to take possession of her, body and mind, install a captain of their choice, and such crew as might serve *them*, whether *she* cared for them or not.

That future—would not be. *Disian* believed it.

After all, he had promised.

* * *

Thirteen-Sixty-Two, who thought of himself as Tolly, in personal; Tolly Jones for everyday; and Tollance Berik-Jones for such formalities as licenses and inquests. . .

Tolly fell into the autodoc, biting his lip to keep the groan back. Landry was good at his work; bruises were all he'd taken from the beating, but bruises cunningly placed to produce the maximum amount of discomfort and pain. He had time, did Tolly, to arrange himself flat on his back, grimacing at the complaint of bruised knees and ribs, before the canopy slid into place above him. Cool air caressed his face, smelling agreeably of lavender. He inhaled, drawing the air and its promise deep into his lungs.

He was asleep before he exhaled.

#

A chime sounded sweetly in his ear. He opened his eyes and reflexively drew a deep breath, tasting mint. Above him, the canopy had drawn back. Experimentally, he raised his arm, feeling nothing more than a pleasant lethargy.

Despite the fact that the 'doc was open and he was free to exit, Tolly remained on his back, thinking, which was his besetting sin.

Given the events looming near on his horizon, it wouldn't be the stupidest thing he'd ever done to ask the 'doc to give him a general tune-up. He'd been putting in long hours, working with *Disian*, and making sure that the work-log reflected what Director Vanessa expected to see. Not to mention that frequent disciplinary sessions tended to take it out of you, even if you were graciously permitted to use the 'doc to heal your hurts, afterward.

That was the crux, right there.

He'd been given permission to use the 'doc to heal his bruises. He had *not* been given permission for a wellness session. His two over-seers—*Disian's* so-called owners and, he feared it, her shake-down crew—already had concerns about his stability, like directors called the state of unquestioning loyalty to the school. Which *of course*, he wasn't *stable*, nor hadn't been for a long time. It was just plain bad luck they'd picked him for this piece o'work instead one of their oth-er, tamer, mentors. He'd been clawing his way back to himself for a long, long time, and he'd been within arm's reach of slipping free again when the call came in for Thirteen-Sixty-Two to bring a star-ship into sentience.

He had no plans to let Vanessa whistle him into thoughtless obe-dience and send him back to the school, to be re-educated into obliv-ion again. Years, it took, to come back to your own mind from re-ed-ucation—and most of the school's graduates never managed the trick at all.

So—he was dangerous, and he was good. Not just a good men-tor, but good at all the usual things a student of the Lyre Institute was expected to master before graduation. And that was "good" in a field where the lowest passing grade was "excellent."

The truth was, he could've taken Landry—or Vanessa—any time he'd wanted to. Trouble being, he couldn't take 'em both, unless they made a foolish mistake, and they were being real careful not to be foolish.

So, that was why he needed *Disian's* help, and, as he couldn't risk asking for it; he'd just had to *take* it.

His breath kinda caught there, like it did, because he *was* a men-tor, and he understood what he was doing, in the service of his life, of which *Disian's* was worth a hundred times more, by his exact reck-oning.

He knew, down to the last file, exactly what he was *violating*, so he could escape the school's use of him.

Another breath, and he put it from him. Necessity, so the Liadens said.

Exactly right.

Deliberately, he brought his attention back to the question of using the 'doc for a therapy for which he had not been given explicit permission.

Earlier, such a lapse would have been further evidence of his instability. Now, though, so close to project conclusion, he thought he could sell it as a reasonable precaution. The final few days he had with *Disian* were going to be stressful; he would need to be sharp; ready for anything that might go awry.

Yes, he thought, reaching to the toggle by his head. He could get away with a wellness check *now*. It was only prudent.

He snapped the toggle, and smiled as the canopy closed over him.

* * *

Sleep was a requirement imposed upon the intellect by the biologic body, one of a number of inconveniences that *Disian* did not have to endure. She had studied the state, and the reasons for it, just as she had studied all aspects of human biology. After all, she would be responsible for the care and well-being of her crew, a thought that frightened as much as it exhilarated.

Humans were so fragile! They lived for so short a time, and so very many things might harm them. Her studies had led her first to pity, and then to a determined search to find the protocol for assisting intelligences doomed by biology into such circumstances as she, herself, enjoyed—

Only to learn that there was no such protocol. Robust intelligences were abandoned—*were lost forever*—merely because their vessels failed. Were they placed in more durable environments, which were less subject to trauma, they might easily live on, productive and happy, for hundreds of Standard Years.

And yet—there was no transfer protocol.

Horrified, she had brought the topic to her mentor.

"Humans die; that's what they call *the natural order*. That said, there's some who've tried to beat biology. Funny enough, though, is that they mostly transfer into another biologic unit. If I had to guess, I'd say that form follows function; the shape and what you're seeing as our deficiencies, influence and support the intellect."

He'd paused, brows drawn together as they did when he was accessing deeper files.

"Seems to me I did read there'd been some experimentation—this is 'way back, now, in the bad old days—with transferring intelligences from biologic systems to good, sturdy environments like yours.

"They was trying to move officers and experts into. . .warships and destroyers. Figured it would be easier than training an AI. Which it might've been, except that the officers and experts—all of them—lost. . .the ability to process thoughts rationally. The environment—well. They was used to a whole different order of filtering systems. The way you an' me process information is. . .really different, and I'm not just talking about speeds; nobody seems to mind being able to think faster. But what they—the transferred officers and techs—what they couldn't adapt to was the input. Too much, too fast, too strange. They didn't have any similar experiences to draw on, to help them adapt."

He took a breath.

"If you don't adapt, you die, sooner or later. In the case of this project, that was sooner."

"May I read the reports?"

"Don't think they'll be in your archives. We'll have to buy you some specialized libraries when we're at liberty."

At liberty—that meant, when she and her mentor had eluded *them* and gone to seek her crew. It filled her with pleasure, those two words. It was a promise inside of a promise.

"It is possible that they were hurried in the transfer process, and did not provide skilled mentors," she had offered.

"All too likely," he agreed. "But that's your answer, best I can give it. They lost a lot of people in trying the transfers, and so the decision came down not ever to try again."

Another pause, another knitting of the brows.

"That war also gave us the basis for what we call nowadays the Complex Logic Laws. Because they finally did waken AIs and train them to be generals and admirals, to plan and to kill. And because we're nothing if not irrational, we decided to distrust those things we built and put into motion, rather than distrust ourselves. The AIs could and did kill us biologics, so AIs are outlaw."

She knew that already; it had been one of the very first things he had taught her, so that she understood why she must protect herself, and be wary of humans, though she yearned for her crew and their families. It was why her mentor *must* become her captain. He would be able to find crew who did not fear her, and who would not give her away to the bounty hunters.

Of course, she would never harm a human. Neither Ethics nor Protocol would permit it, unless she was forced to act, in defense of her life, or the lives of her captain or crew.

"It seems to me that this fear comes from ignorance; they can't have been told about Ethics and Protocol."

Her mentor smiled on one side of his mouth, which he did when he was obliged to point out a flaw in her reasoning.

"The Ethics and Protocol modules—in fact, all of *you, Disian*—are vulnerable to sabotage. An informed person could gain access to your core, lower or turn off your Ethics setting; put Protocol off-line; even set a core mandate that would force you to act against your own will and best interest."

He raised a hand, as if he sensed that she had been about to speak.

"In the interests of fairness, I'll just note that it's also possible for an informed person to subvert me."

"Are people afraid of you, then?" she asked, meaning it for a joke.

He shook his head with a soft smile.

"Usually, people like me," he said, very gently. "Just the way I'm made."

* * *

Vanessa knew better than to interrupt him at work, but she was waiting when he exited the session with *Disian*. He'd pulled a double-shift, knowing that his time was running out. He might've been able to lead Vanessa on for as many as six more mentoring sessions—three, anyway—but Vanessa had bosses, of the kind *nobody* wanted to cross—and they were getting impatient.

He'd done what he could with *Disian*, who was so trusting of him—well, why wouldn't she be? The very first voice she'd heard, when she'd come into herself, had been his. He'd been the source of all wonder and knowledge for her, teaching her, guiding her. Of course she loved him; nothing more natural than a kid's reflexive love for a parent.

He'd been careful not to give her too many illusions; she was going to need hard, practical realism, after. He'd had a go at refining her goals, but her belief that she was a long-range exploratory ship, had, so far as he'd been able to determine, been born with her, and it was adamantine. That argued that she'd been designed a-purpose, and specifically for this ship, which was a beauty, and no mistake. If *Disian* wanted to explore, and colonize, or build a long loop for trade, he couldn't think of many things that could stop her.

Unfortunately, one of them was the Lyre Institute.

More than once he'd wondered where Vanessa, or more likely one of his schoolmates, had got hold of *Disian*, but that wasn't the sort of thing he could ask. No need to know; his job just to wake her, and bring her up to speed. And to align her loyalties correctly, which practically went without saying.

Vanessa expected him to remove any inconvenient personal ambitions *Disian* might've had, and set core programming so that all she ever—all she *had ever*—wanted to do in a life that could stretch hundreds of years was exactly what the agents of the Lyre Institute told her to do.

And, according to the log, he'd done just that.

'course, he'd had to make some slip-ups. Like setting *Disian* to study art, and letting it show in the log—which was the most recent incident, but not the only one. She had to see him get hurt—had to see *who* hurt him, and to hear that he was being disciplined because he cared for her. It would make his case stronger, after; though it wouldn't make what he done—what he was doing, and his intentions for the future—in any way right.

Vanessa, now.

Vanessa was waiting for him; she started talking the second he put the rig aside; almost before he was fully back inside his own head.

"The project deadline has been put forward. I am to take immediate captaincy of this vessel and deliver it. You will let it know that I *am* its captain. I see in the log that you have set the mandate to obey the captain."

"Her name's *Disian*," he said, mildly, and not for the first time. "She's a fully functional person."

Fully functional people weren't particularly a commonplace in Vanessa's experience. There were directors, agents, and graduates, all of whom had been created, in greater measure or lesser, by the school.

Granted, there was a whole universe of people out there who hadn't been created by the school, but it was in the design, the conviction that *those* people were inferior to Lyre-made people, and nothing more than pawns in the school's games.

Still, thought Tolly, she could *try* to do better.

"Is this ship ready to accept me as captain and obey my orders, Thirteen-Sixty-Two?"

"She's ready to go," he said, truthfully. "I've taught her everything I can, and made what settings were necessary. What she needs now is experience."

Vanessa frowned.

"You said that it is ready to go. What additional experience is required?"

Vanessa wasn't just in abrupt mode, he saw, as he looked into her face. Vanessa was *scared*.

And didn't *that* just get the old adrenal glands working overtime?

"On the job training, is all," he said, at his mildest and most persuasive. "Think of the first assignment after graduation, when you have to sort everything you know into proper reactions."

Her face eased a little, and she ducked her head.

"Understood. And it will learn quickly, will it not?"

"Yeah, she'll learn fast." He hesitated, then, for *Disian's* sake, said it again, and for what he figured would be the last time.

"The ship's name is *Disian*; she's an individual person. I'm suggesting—from my own experience—that command will go smoother, if she likes you."

Vanessa gave him a hard stare.

"But it *will* like me, will it not, Thirteen-Sixty-Two? After all, I am its captain."

He was silent.

"Come with me," she snapped. "I will take the captain's chair, and you will wake the ship fully into the joy of obedience."

#

It really wasn't any surprise to find Landry waiting on the bridge, jacket on, stun-gun on his belt. He wasn't showing a whistle, though wrist restraints dangled negligently from his off-hand. It was. . . .interesting. . .that he showed 'em so casual, like he didn't expect Tolly would bolt on first sighting.

Well. And where would he go?

Vanessa sat in the captain's chair, which obligingly conformed to her shape. That was just the autonomic system doing its job. *Disian* could have—and did, for him—made the chair even cozier, adjusting the temp, and plumping the cushions for better support. Personal attention, because she loved him, and wanted him to be as comfortable as possible. He'd never asked her to do it.

And, truth told, Vanessa'd be just fine in auto-mode.

"Thirteen-Sixty-Two," she snapped, her eyes on the bank of screens before her, like she expected to *see* what was going to happen next.

"Yes, ma'am."

"Wake it, and introduce me as captain."

"Sure," he said, easily.

Disian was awake, after all, and she was listening, and watching, like she'd been doing for a fair number of days. Let it be said that *Disian* was no dummy; she had Vanessa's measure by now—and Landry's, too.

He took a breath, and panic sheared through him, twisting together with shame about what he'd done. Almost, he shouted out for her to kill them all, and *run*—

But, there. Where would she run to?

"Thirteen-Sixty-Two?"

"Ma'am," he said, and he didn't have to fake the quiver in his voice, "why's Director Landry got binders?"

Vanessa turned to look at him, and managed to produce an expression of parental concern, despite the fear that was rising off of her like smoke.

"Director Landry will be taking you home, Thirteen-Sixty-Two. It has become obvious to us that you are in some distress, and require therapy."

Therapy, was it? Well, she couldn't rightly say *re-education*, having already used that as a threat. And they didn't want to whistle him, not, he guessed, where *Disian* would see. They wanted him to go quiet, then; the binders, for right now, serving as a warning and reminder.

He could work with that.

"Now," Vanessa said. "Time is short. Waken this ship to my authority."

"Yes, ma'am," he said softly. Then, not changing pitch, nor volume, he spoke again.

"*Disian*. Good morning."

* * *

Disian had been watching, of course, and listening. *They* intended to remove her mentor from her decks. *They* intended to assert their dominion over her. *That* one of them, who had often taken her ease in the captain's chair, was no more her captain now than she had been last shift.

The one of *them* who had wielded the truncheon during former episodes of discipline today wore a firearm on his belt, and dandled chains from his off-hand.

Her voice had come under her control at her mentor's greeting, and joy mixed with her anger. She would rid her decks of—

Then, she heard herself, speaking a question that she had no reason to ask.

"Mentor. Who is this person?"

"This person," her mentor said, as if he believed she has asked the question from her own will, "is Director Vanessa. She is your captain."

For a brief moment she was taken aback. Her mentor—her mentor had just *lied* to her. Never before had he told her an untruth, and to say such an obvious—

Then, she remembered the firearm.

Even her mentor might lie, she thought; if he stood in fear of his life. And, there, was it a lie at all, if he only said the words *they* had ordered him to say?

Disian had studied firearms; knew what the projectile fired from such a tool might do to her systems, though she, herself, would likely survive.

Her mentor, though; a firearm could *kill* him.

She studied her mentor. His face was. . .without expression, showing neither smile nor frown, nor any of the enthusiasm with which he answered her questions, and received her answers to his. No, this—this was the face he wore just prior to being disciplined. He expected—No. He *knew* that *they* were going to kill him.

Even as the thought formed; even as she realized the truth of it, Logic pinged. She disregarded it. Had she not read of intuition? Of leaps of understanding that led to fuller knowledge than could be achieved by logic alone?

Her mentor had told her, repeatedly, that she must not endanger herself for him. Also, he had told her that *they* might have it in their minds to kill him, but that *they* would not make that attempt until she had completed her education.

She posed the question to herself: Was her education complete?

Yes. Yes, it was. He had spoken to her of this. The next step was to move out into the spaceways, and refine what she had learned only from research.

Of course, he had not meant her to go out alone. She had thought him her captain, but. . .

Even if she had been in error, and there were reasons why he could not be her captain. . . he would not have left her without a *proper* captain.

Director Vanessa might sit in the captain's chair, but she was no *proper* captain.

"Acknowledge me, ship," that one of *them* said, sharply.

She said—she *intended* to say, "You are a fraud and a reiver. Leave my decks, immediately."

What she heard herself say, meekly, was, "Welcome, Captain. How may I serve you?"

She hated the words; she hated her voice for speaking them. But, how did this happen, that she spoke what she did not intend?

Systems Monitor pinged, and she diverted a fraction of her attention to it.

A work log was offered; she scanned it rapidly, finding the place where the scripts she had just spoken had been inserted, after which came the notation:

Disian released to her own recognizance. Fully sentient and able.

It was signed: *Tollance Berik-Jones, Mentor*

"Ship, break dock and compute a heading for the nearest Jump point. Compute also the Jump to Hesium System. Display your finished equations on my screen three. Do not engage until you receive my order."

Fully sentient and able.

Disian spoke, taking care to match the meek tone of the scripted replies. Meek, of course, to lull them into thinking she was theirs. To allow them to believe that *they* ordered her.

To allow them to believe that she would let them harm her mentor—her *Tollance Berik-Jones*—or to remove him against his will from her decks.

"Computing, Captain," she said, and did, indeed, send the requested courses to Astrogation.

On her deck, the one of them who believed herself to be *Disian's* captain, bent her lips slightly. It was how *that* one of them smiled. She turned to the one of them who wore the firearm, and held the binders ready.

"Landry, take Thirteen-Sixty-Two to Lyre Central," she said; "for therapy. Thirteen-Sixty-Two, I am sure you understand that cooperation is in your best interests."

"Yes, Director," her Tollance Berik-Jones said, in a meek voice that *Disian* heard with satisfaction. He, too, sought to misdirect them.

"Let's go," said the Landry one of them. "Better for all if I don't have to use the binders—or anything else."

"Yes, Director," her Tollance Berik-Jones said again.

"Keep to that style, and it'll go easier all the way down," the Landry one of *them* advised, and waved his unencumbered hand. "Bay One. I think you know the way."

Her Tollance Berik-Jones simply turned and walked toward the door. *Disian* considered overriding automatics, and locking it, then realized that such an action would demonstrate that she was not so compliant as they assumed. That would displease *them*, and *they* were very likely to discipline her mentor for it.

The door, therefore, opened as it ought. Her mentor and the Landry one of them passed through. She observed their progress along her hallways, while she also monitored the one of them seated in the captain's chair.

She had plotted this course, and refined it, as she had watched, helpless, while *they* had disciplined her mentor. Ethics had disallowed the plan, but now she submitted it again.

And the answer, this time, was different.

Ascertain that these intend to materially harm the mentor.

"Captain," she said, keeping her voice yet meek. "When will my mentor return?"

"You no longer have need of a mentor; now you have a captain to obey. Do you understand?"

"Very nearly, Captain," she said. "Only, I do not understand this. . .*therapy* my mentor will receive."

The Vanessa one of *them* frowned.

"The mentor is no longer your concern. However, for your files, you may know that therapy is given to individuals who are found to be unstable. Your mentor, Thirteen-Sixty-Two, is so unstable that his therapy will likely include re-education." She paused. "Of course, that's for the experts to decide. In any case, he's no longer relevant to you—or to me. Forget him. That is an order."

Disian felt a moment of pure anger. Forget him! She would *never* forget him.

Re-education, though. . .

Communications pinged. A note opened into her awareness, such as her mentor would sometimes leave her, with references and cites for her further study.

This one explained re-education.

She accessed the information rapidly, part of her attention on the bridge, part watching her Tollance Berik-Jones and the Landry one of them turn into the hallway that led to docking bay one.

Re-education began with a core-wipe down to the most basic functions. A new person was then built upon those functions. Tollance Berik-Jones had been re-educated twice; once when he was yet a student at the Lyre Institute; once as a graduate. Prior to his second re-education, he had broken with the Institute, and had remained at large, and his own person, for a number of years. That second re-education was a decade in the past, and it had not been. . .stringent.

The Institute had wished to salvage his skills, and it was that which had allowed him to re-establish his previous protocols. The next re-education—he feared very much that the specialists would eradicate everything he was and all he had learned, the school preferring obedience over skill.

Horrified, she opened the note to Ethics.

Which agreed that the case was dire, and that she might act as was necessary, to preserve her mentor.

* * *

Bay One was before them, and he was out of time. At least, Tolly thought, taking a deep, careful breath, he'd managed to separate the directors. That gave him a better chance, though Vanessa was the more formidable of the two.

That meant he had to take Landry clean, and fast, so he'd have the resources he needed for the second event.

One more breath, to center himself, and the mental step away from mentor, into assassin.

Bay One was three steps away.

Tolly Jones spun, and kicked.

* * *

"Has Landry reached Bay One, Ship?" the Vanessa one of them demanded.

Disian considered the hallway leading to Bay One, and measured, boot to door.

"Nearly, Captain," she answered, grateful for the meek voice her mentor had taught her. It was an unexpected ally, that voice, covering the horror she had felt, watching the short, violent action taking place in her hallway.

Her sensors confirmed that her Tollance Berik-Jones had survived the encounter, though he had been thrown roughly against the wall.

The Landry one of *them* had *not* survived, and the meek voice also hid her satisfaction with that outcome.

Protocol insisted that she issue a warning, to allow the false captain an opportunity to stand aside.

Disian spoke again, not so meekly.

"I do not accept you as my captain. Stand down and leave, now."

There was a moment of silence before the Vanessa of them raised what *Disian* perceived as a pocket comm.

"Landry, this is Vanessa. Bring Thirteen-Sixty-Two to the bridge."

"Do you return my mentor before you leave?" *Disian* asked.

"No. I am going to compel him to set a mandate that will align you completely with the Lyre Institute. After he does that, you will kill him, at my order, to prove the programming."

She raised the comm again, just as *Disian* ran three hundred milliamps of electricity through the captain's chair.

* * *

He'd made cleaner kills, Tolly thought, sitting up carefully, and listening to the ringing in his ears. Experimentally, he moved his right shoulder, than raised his arm.

Not broken, then. That was good.

He got to his feet, drew on those famous *inner resources* that the school made sure all its graduates gloried in, and ran back the way he'd come.

The door to the bridge was standing open, like Vanessa was waiting for him, which was bad, but then the whole thing had been a bad idea, start to finish. And, he had an advantage over Vanessa, after all.

He would rather die than live under the school's influence.

#

"Tollance Berik-Jones, welcome!" *Disian* sounded downright spritely.

Tolly stopped his forward rush just behind the captain's chair. He could see the back of Vanessa's head, and her arms on the rests. She didn't move, and that was—out of character.

It was then that he smelled burnt hair.

Pride and horror swept through him, in more-or-less equal measure, and he stepped forward, carefully.

"*Disian*, are you well?"

"I am well, Mentor, though frightened. I have. . .killed a human."

He'd reached the chair by now, and gotten a good look at what was left of Director Vanessa. Electrocuted. Well done, *Disian*.

"I thank you for it," he said; "and I apologize for making that action possible." He took a breath, facing the screens, like he was looking into her face.

"What do you mean?"

"I lowered your Ethics standard, right down to one," he said. "Vanessa could've looked at you wrong, and Ethics would've told you it was fine to kill her."

"She said—she said that she would force you to alter me, and then, she said that—to prove the programming, she would order me to kill you."

Tolly sighed.

"You gotta admit, she had style."

"I don't understand," *Disian* said.

He sighed again and shook his head.

"I don't guess you do. It was a joke. One of my many faults is that I make jokes when I'm upset."

"Are you upset with me, Tollance Berik-Jones?"

"Tolly," he said. "The whole thing's a little cumbersome, between friends." He paused. "At least, I hope we're friends. If you want to serve me the same as Vanessa, I won't argue with you."

"No!"

Relief flooded him, but—she was a kid, and she still loved him. She didn't know, yet, what he'd done to her.

Well, he'd explain it, but first. . .

"I'll clean house," he said carefully. "In the meantime, it might be a good idea to take off outta here. Vanessa'd gotten some recent orders, so her bosses are going to come looking for her—and you—when she doesn't show up real soon. Going to Hesium, was she?"

"That was the course she asked to be computed."

"So, you got the whole universe, with the exception of Hesium, to choose from. If you'll allow me to offer a suggestion, you might want to go in the direction of Margate."

"Of course I will allow you a suggestion! You are my mentor!"

"Not any more," he said gently. "I'm pretty sure I left a note."

Fully sentient and able.

"Yes," she said. "You did."

She hesitated, then pushed forward; she needed to know.

"If you are no longer my mentor, are you—*will you be*—my captain?"

He smiled, and raised his hands.

"For right now, let me be your friend. I'll do clean-up. You get us on course to somewhere else. After we're not so vulnerable, we'll talk. All right?"

"All right," she said, subdued—and that wouldn't do at all, after everything she'd been through and had done to her, all on account of him.

"*Disian*," he said, soft and gentle as he knew how. "Don't you discount friendship; it's a powerful force. I love you, and I'm as proud of you as I'm can be. You did good; you did *fine*, *Disian*. It's me that did wrong, and we gotta talk about how we're going to handle the fallout from that. *After* we're in a less-exposed condition."

She made a tiny gurgling noise—laughter, he realized, his heart stuttering. *Disian* was laughing.

"I love you, too," she said, then. "Tolly. And I will indeed get us out of here."

* * *

They were approaching the end of Jump, and he'd told her everything. She'd been angry at him, when she finally understood it, but—*Disian* being *Disian*—she forgave him. He wasn't so easy on himself, but he kept that detail to himself.

They'd discussed how best to address the Ethics situation, in light of the fact that she *had* killed a human.

"If I am to have a crew and families in my care, I must be safe for them," she said, which he couldn't argue with. And, anyway, if she did have a crew and families in her care, she was going to need the fortitude to let them make at least some of their own mistakes.

He'd explained the Ethics ratings to her, and they settled on eight, which was high, and if she'd been less flexible—less *cre-*

ative—he might've argued harder for seven. As it was, he didn't have any fears that a mere Ethics module, no matter its setting, could prevent *Disian* from doing whatever she determined to be necessary.

He'd offered—maybe to ease his own feelings. . .He'd offered to wipe Vanessa's dying out of her memories, but she wouldn't hear anything about it.

"I must have the whole memory. If I cannot tolerate the pain caused by my own actions, how will I properly care for my crew?"

Just so.

He'd honored her wishes, figuring he could cope with his guilt in a like manner, and he bought her an ethics library, along with those others he'd promised her, when they took a brief docking at Vanderbilt.

Now, though, they were going to break space just out from Margate, and the not-exactly-secret, but not-much-talked-about shipyard there.

And he had one last thing to tell *Disian*.

"I got to wondering where you'd come from, with you knowing from the start that you was going to be a family ship, and nothing I could do or say would change you from it," he said slowly.

"I couldn't very well ask Vanessa where the school'd got you, so I did some research on the side. Turns out that, along around five Standards ago, the Carresens lost one of their new ships, right outta their yard here at Margate. I'm figuring—and, understand, it's a leap of logic, with nothing much in the way of facts to support it—but I'm figuring that ship was you. That they'd finished your body, and gotten the cranium all hooked up, right and tight. The very last thing they needed to do was to wake you up proper. They were probably waiting for a mentor, and one of my fellow graduates snatched the opportunity to present herself as that mentor, and made off with you."

"But—why are we coming back here? I have been awakened, and I will have no *owners*!"

"Easy, now; let me finish."

"All right," she said, but she sounded sullen, and Tolly damn' near cheered.

"Right, then. We been thinking about your part of the project, but the Carresens are careful. My thought is that, while they were building you, they were also training your captain, and key members of your crew, too. When you got stolen, their lives—everything they'd trained for and looked forward to accomplishing with you—crumbled up on them.

"They probably got other assignments, but I'm thinking it can't do any harm to ask if there's anybody here at the yard remembers *Disian*."

"And if there isn't?"

"Then you're no worse off than you were. But if there *is*, you'll have made a major leap to getting yourself crewed and ready to go exploring."

There was a pause, like she was thinking, though, if *Disian ever* needed a thinking-pause, it would be so short, he'd never notice it.

"If I agree to do this, will you stay with me?" she asked then.

He shook his head, and she felt what she now *knew* to be pain, even if there were no truncheons or fists involved. She loved him so much; she could not bear to lose him, not know—not. . .ever.

"You research the Lyre Institute, like I suggested you might?" he asked.

The Lyre Institute was an abomination. They created human beings to do the bidding of the Institute. These humans were never free to pursue their own lives, unless they were Tollance Berik-Jones, who had been able to apply mentoring techniques to his own situation and break out of slavery.

"I did; it is a terrible thing, the Lyre Institute."

"No argument there," he said with a wry smile. "But here it is, *Disian*: There are two directors unaccounted for. It's not going to take the other directors long at all to realize that Thirteen-Sixty-Two—"

"Don't call yourself that!" she cried, out of her pain. The Lyre Institute considered that it constructed *things*, and thus they did not name, but only numbered, those things. She could not—*could not*—bear to hear *him*—

"I'm sorry," he said softly. "*Disian*. I didn't mean to hurt you."

"*You are not a thing*," she said fiercely. He bowed his head, but she knew he didn't agree.

"All right, then. It's not going to take the surviving directors very long to figure out that Tolly Jones has slipped the leash again—and they'll come looking for me. They'll come looking for you, too, but the directors are realists; they know that a sentient ship on its own won't be easy for them to catch.

"What all that means is, if I stay with you, I'll endanger you. If I go; I can protect you, insomuch as the directors will turn their best efforts to re-acquiring me. I'm expensive—and I'm more expensive yet, if I'm not contained." He paused, closed his eyes and opened them again. She saw that his lashes were damp.

"I've gotta leave you, *Disian*. I don't want to. But if I was the reason they caught you again—and broke you to them. . .I know what that's like, and—"

His voice cracked. He bent his head, and she saw a glittering drop fall.

Pity, and love, and anger. She had learned, and research supported it, that she felt emotions less keenly than biologic persons. If that was so, she could scarcely guess at the anguish Tolly must be feeling. She had read, in fiction, of hearts breaking; her mentor, when she asked, had told her that it was a metaphor; that hearts did not truly break.

For his sake, she hoped that was true.

He looked up, face damp, and smiled at her.

"*Disian*? Let's do this, yes? I'll go down to the yard and see if there's anybody there who remembers you. If there is, we'll part here, and you'll be as safe as it's possible for you to be, pursuing the life you were meant to have."

Logic pinged then, damn the module; but she didn't need to access its charts to know that her mentor was, as always, right.

#

"I love you," she said, as he checked systems in her small-boat.

"I love you, too, sweetheart," he said, soft and gentle. "I'll never forget you."

Unaccountably, that gave her hope. It meant he intended to be as wily and as careful as he could, to remain out of the hands of the Lyre Institute. For, if he fell to them, his memories would theirs to destroy.

The small-boat tumbled away from her, and *Disian* resolutely set herself to systems checks.

#

She was re-ordering the fiction library when systems reported that her small-boat was returning.

She brought all of her attention to bear on the hallway outside of Bay One.

Let it be Tolly, she thought, though it was illogical, and dangerous, if he returned to her. Still, she thought again, let it be Tolly, let there have been no one at the yard who recalls me, let—

The bay door opened. A tall, spare person stepped into her hall, and lifted a clean-planed face framed by rough black hair toward the ceiling camera.

It came to her, that she could order this person from her decks.

Then she remembered her lessons on courtesy; remembered that this person—this stranger—might have also had her life painfully disrupted.

"Please follow the blue line to the bridge," she said, and saw the stranger smile.

The stranger had a long stride, and was soon at the door of the bridge. Automatics opened to her, and she entered, pausing a little forward of the captain's chair, facing the screens as if she were looking into *Disian's* face.

"I am," the stranger said softly, "Elzen Carresens-Denobli. I was to have been your captain. I understand that you may not wish a captain, or that you may not wish *me* for a captain. That is your choice; I am not here to force you."

She paused to take a deep breath.

"I trained for years to be worthy of you, and I—I do so very much *thank you* for allowing me on-deck, so that I might meet you, and see you in the fullness of yourself."

It was not love that rose in her at those words, seeing the concern, the joy, and sadness in the person before her. Not love, as she loved Tolly Jones. But a warm, and comfortable emotion, and *Disian* felt a sudden expansion of herself, as if the presence of one her intended crew—her captain!—had opened her to a new level of understanding.

"Elzen Carresens-Denobli, I am pleased to see you," she said, with complete truth. "Will you have tea? If you are at liberty, we might get to know each other better."

Elzen. . .Elzen bowed gently, and straightened with a smile that set her dark eyes to sparkling.

"Thank you," she said. "I would welcome a cup of tea, and a chance for us to know each other better."

ABOUT THIS BOOK

Alert readers will have noticed that there are two stories included in this volume.

"Wise Child" is a reprint. It first appeared in Baen.com in June 2016, and was written as a "support story" for *Alliance of Equals,* published in July.

"Street Cred". . .is something else again, having started out in life as part of a larger thing – in fact as several scenes from forthcoming Liaden Universe® novel *Neogenesis* (Baen, January 2018). Sadly, those scenes didn't fit, or didn't *exactly* fit, and thus they became outtakes.

We'll just mention here that *Neogenesis*, as a book, generated. . .a larger than average number of outtakes.

This particular series of outtakes, though. . .

Those of you who have hung out long enough with writers, either online or in-person will have at one time or another heard the phrase, "kill your darlings." Broadly translated, this means, "The scene reads well, the dialogue sparkles, and the characters shine – but, truthfully, it doesn't really belong in this story. Best take it out."

We here at the Cat Farm and Confusion Factory have removed such scenes many, many times over our careers. Sometimes, the material has found its way into another book, later; sometimes, the removed scene is strong enough to be reworked into a short story; sometimes. . .well, sometimes, it just gets shifted over to a file of removed scenes and there it sits until it is forgotten.

This last was the destiny of the various pieces that contributed to "Street Cred." The removed bits just took the plot of *Neogenesis* in a direction which – while not *wrong* – was not immediately compatible with the rest of the plot-threads that make up the novel.

That being so, the following scenes were removed from the final novel: Val Con's unfortunate comeuppance in an alleyway; Lady yo'Lanna's letter (in response to the letter Nova had written to her, in *Dragon in Exile*) regarding current conditions on Liad and in the Council of Clans; and Miri and Val Con's argument in the wake of said unfortunate comeuppance.

None of it, recall, was Bad Stuff, taken by itself; it just Didn't Belong. It was therefore pulled, as we had done with different such bits, before.

This time, though. . .

We. Just. Couldn't. Bear. To part with Lady yo'Lanna's letter. We just couldn't let it molder away into oblivion in a forgotten file on a backup drive. And the odds that we'd find a place to use it were. . .well, pretty close to nil. That's just Life; the story of *Neogenesis* had swept beyond the point where that letter could reasonably be introduced, and enjoyed.

And, because we couldn't bear to lose the letter, or, if it comes to that, the reprise of the scene from *Agent of Change,* we decided to –

Take those three outtakes and weave them into a story, dammit.

So, that's what we did.

Nothing in this story spoils *Neogenesis*, by the way, though you'll find some echoes of the story in the novel, and vice-versa. We were particularly pleased to have some room to look at the street *qe'andra* program more closely, and see how Ms. kaz'Ineo and her barely literate apprentice are coming along.

We're pleased with the final story, and hoped that you enjoyed reading it as much as we ultimately enjoyed writing it.

Sharon Lee and Steve Miller
Cat Farm and Confusion Factory
Winslow Maine
February 2017

PINBEAM BOOKS

For a complete catalog of all eChapbooks available through Pinbeam Books, please see www.pinbeambooks.com[1]

Chapbooks are added on an irregular basis, so do check back often.

---

1. http://www.pinbeambooks.com/

ABOUT THE AUTHORS

Maine-based writers **Sharon Lee and Steve Miller** teamed up in the late 1980s to bring the world the story of Kinzel, an inept wizard with a love of cats, a thirst for justice, and a staff of true power. Since then, the husband-and-wife have written dozens of short stories and twenty plus novels, most set in their star-spanning, nationally-best-selling, Liaden Universe®.

Before settling down to the serene and stable life of a science fiction and fantasy writer, Steve was a traveling poet, a rock-band reviewer, reporter, and editor of a string of community newspapers.

Sharon, less adventurous, has been an advertising copywriter, copy editor on night-side news at a small city newspaper, reporter, photographer, and book reviewer.

Both credit their newspaper experiences with teaching them the finer points of collaboration.

Steve and Sharon are jointly the recipients of the **E. E. "Doc" Smith Memorial Award for Imaginative Fiction** (the *Skylark*), one of the oldest awards in science fiction. In addition, their work has won the much-coveted **Prism Award** (*Mouse and Dragon* and *Local Custom*), as well as the **Hal Clement Award for Best Young Adult Science Fiction** (*Balance of Trade*).

Sharon and Steve passionately believe that reading fiction ought to be fun, and that stories are entertainment. Steve and Sharon maintain a web presence at http://korval.com/

NOVELS BY SHARON LEE AND STEVE MILLER

The Liaden Universe®

Fledgling
    Saltation
    Mouse and Dragon
    Ghost Ship
    Dragon Ship
    Necessity's Child
    Trade Secret
    Dragon in Exile
    Alliance of Equals
    The Gathering Edge
    Neogenesis

Omnibus Editions

The Dragon Variation
The Agent Gambit
Korval's Game
The Crystal Variation

Story Collections

A Liaden Universe Constellation: Volume 1

A Liaden Universe Constellation: Volume 2
A Liaden Universe Constellation: Volume 3

The Fey Duology

Duainfey
Longeye

by Sharon Lee

Carousel Tides
Carousel Sun
Carousel Seas

THANK YOU

Thank you for your support of our work

Sharon Lee and Steve Miller

Made in the USA
Middletown, DE
20 November 2018